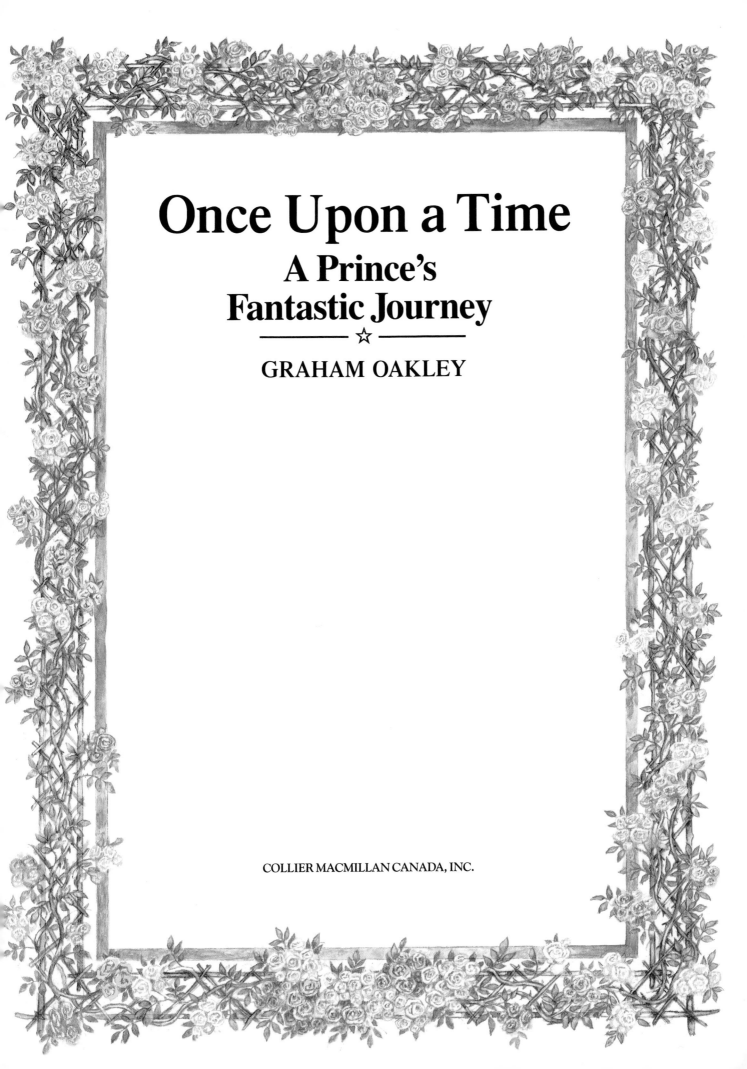

Once Upon a Time

A Prince's
Fantastic Journey

———— ☆ ————

GRAHAM OAKLEY

COLLIER MACMILLAN CANADA, INC.

I'm a page in the Royal palace and my name is Clarence. But the Lord Chamberlain always calls me "You grubby little tyke" and somehow it's caught on. It's a bit of a mouthful, though, so most people just call me Tyke.

On the morning this story really began, the Lord Chamberlain grabbed me by the ear and said, "Tomorrow morning, Prince Alfred is setting off on a journey. He'll need a page, so I'm giving him you. That'll get you out of my hair for a few weeks, you perambulating little rubbish heap. Pack your things and be sure you're ready to start at eight sharp tomorrow morning."

So at eight o'clock the next morning I was ready and waiting at the front door of the palace. Prince Alfred showed up at eleven in a very bad temper – his farewell party was still going on and he didn't want to leave it. He did manage a smile for the TV cameras as we set off, though.

But the fresh air and exercise soon put him in a better mood.

"You're jolly lucky to be my page," he said chattily. "You see, I'm being sent on this trip to perform three tasks. The first is to prove that I'm clever; the second, to find a girl who'll make a good queen; and the third is to prove that I'm brave. If, or rather when, I've done all that my old man has promised to retire and then I'll be King. If you've been a good page, I'll make you my Equerry and that means that one day, what with all the perks, you'll be rich."

So it looked as if my fortune was made. *If* all went well that is. Tasks two and three should go well enough, but, if what I'd heard about Prince Alfred was true, task number one could be a problem.

Anyway, we hadn't gone far before Prince Alfred decided that walking was beneath a prince's dignity so at the next garage he bought a little car and we went on in that.

Soon we came to a big flyover. Prince Alfred said that signs like NO ENTRY and KEEP LEFT didn't apply to Royalty so he just ignored them. Pretty soon we were in trouble. If we hadn't managed to swerve down a funny little side road our journey would have come to a sticky end there and then.

It didn't take me long to spot that there was something very strange about the place this little road had taken us to. Prince Alfred didn't notice because he was too busy pretending to be a racing driver; he just tore along without ever glancing at a signpost. Thankfully I did, and that was why I was ready for all the curious things that started happening to us.

At mid-day we stopped to eat our packed lunch and then we went exploring. We came across a very high hedge and scrambled through it to see what was on the other side. There was a palace and, as everything was quiet, we went in and wandered about. Even a little kid could have guessed where we were; Prince Alfred didn't though.

At last we came to a little turret room and there was the girl, lying asleep, just as I'd expected.

"That's the Sleeping Beauty, sir," I explained. "She's had a spell put on her by a wicked fairy and she'll sleep for a hundred years unless a prince, *like you*, sir, gives her a kiss." He didn't seem to take the hint so I dropped a heavier one, "She looks the sort of girl who'd *make a good queen*, sir," I said.

"What utter bilge you do talk, Tyke," he snapped. "This is one of those Disneyland places. Come on, let's get out quick before somebody wants to see our tickets."

By the next day we'd nearly run out of petrol and couldn't get any more because Prince Alfred had gone and lost his wallet.

"We'll just have to keep an eye open for some other kind of transport that doesn't need petrol," he said.

That afternoon we saw just the thing. Prince Alfred said he was all for encouraging new technology, so he'd give the lady's invention a whirl and if it was any good he'd swop the car for it.

I said he'd better be careful because the lady looked like a witch and witches can be quite tricky.

"Rubbish," said Prince Alfred. "There are no such things as witches and even if there were I'd jolly well like to see one who could put anything over on me." He didn't have to wait very long.

So now we had neither car nor money and we were getting hungry, too. For days we ate nothing but the few scraps we happened to come across.

One day, while we were resting by the side of the road, Prince Alfred found an old oil lamp in the grass. We were just wondering how much we could sell it for when a pedlar went by shouting, "New lamps for old." That jogged my memory.

"I think we've found Aladdin's magic lamp," I cried. "If you rub it, sir, a genie might come out and grant you three wishes. You could ask him to carry out the tasks, it would save an awful lot of time and trouble, sir."

"Oh, don't talk twaddle, Tyke," said Prince Alfred, and he took the lamp across to the pedlar. After a few minutes haggling they did a deal.

As we rode away Prince Alfred was looking very pleased with himself. "I'll bet even that old genie of yours couldn't have got us transport as quickly as I did just then," he said smugly.

At that moment there was a terrific flash of light and, glancing back, we saw a very surprising thing. For the rest of that day Prince Alfred was rather quiet.

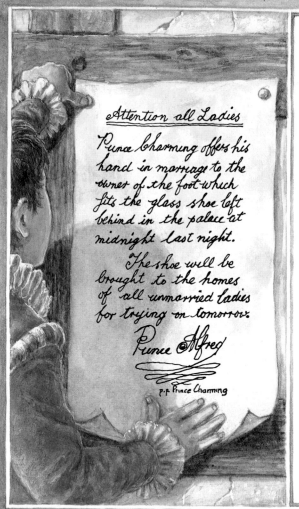

The next morning we arrived at the doors of a palace. Above the bell it said "The Residence of Prince Charming". Prince Alfred rang it because he thought it would be nice to say hello to a fellow prince.

We were asked to stay for a day or two and the butler showed us up to the guest suite. After we'd settled in Prince Alfred went off for a glass of sherry and a chat with Prince Charming.

"Got a terrific idea," he said when he came back. "Prince thingummy met a girl he really fancied at his ball last night, but the funny thing was that while he was chatting her up, she suddenly looked at the clock, gave a shriek and dashed off, shedding a glass slipper as she went. Prince whatsisname's dead keen to marry her, only nobody knows who she is. That's where my idea comes in. If I could find her, it'd show I'm pretty smart and the first task would be in the bag."

The penny hadn't dropped so I started to tell him about Cinderella, but he said, "Sssh, can't you see I'm busy," so I thought I'd try again later.

After half an hour he handed me a piece of paper he'd been writing on.

"That should do the trick," he said. I read it and saw that somehow he'd managed to get on the right track so I left it at that.

Then we went off to explain the plan to Prince Charming.

"Terrific," he said. "Exactly what I always do. I'll leave you to carry on then and I'll have a day off. A chap gets fed up with all those feet over the years." That made Prince Alfred scratch his head, but then he shrugged and told me to go and pin up the notice he'd written where everybody could see it.

We started visiting all the houses early the next morning. We hadn't been to many before Prince Alfred dropped the glass slipper and smashed it. We soon found another but it looked a little bigger to me. I mentioned this to Prince Alfred but he told me not to fuss over details and we continued on our rounds. Before long we found a foot that fitted the slipper exactly. The only snag was the foot didn't belong to Cinderella; it belonged to one of her step-sisters.

I tried to point out the error to Prince Alfred but he was too excited to listen. When we got back to the palace he rushed straight to Prince Charming and told him that he'd found the girl.

"Super," said Prince Charming, without looking up from his newspaper. "We'll have the wedding tomorrow, perhaps you'll make the arrangements as you seem to know the story so well."

Prince Alfred looked slightly puzzled but said, "Certainly, old boy, anything to oblige," and before I could have another go at explaining things he dashed off to start organising the wedding. So now it was up to me to sort things out by myself.

That afternoon I borrowed a nice white dress from a lady-in-waiting's room and took it to Cinderella in her kitchen. I told her to put it on in the morning, slip across to the hall where the wedding was to take place and stand where Prince Charming was sure to see her. She said she wouldn't because that didn't happen in the story. I said that Prince Charming didn't marry an Ugly Sister in the story either but he jolly well would if she didn't do as I asked.

That persuaded her. On the wedding morning she followed my instructions to the letter and it all worked perfectly. There was a bit of a fuss but the wedding took place and Cinderella was the bride, as usual.

After the ceremony, Prince Charming came over and shook Prince Alfred's hand. "Everything was absolutely super, old boy," he cried. "That touch of drama was pure inspiration. Best wedding me and Cinders have had for centuries. Between you and me, it was all getting rather boring, but you really put some fizz back into it. What can I do to thank you?"

Prince Alfred didn't reply, he just stood there looking as if he was trying to do a hard sum in his head, so I spoke up and said that all the worry of the wedding arrangements had numbed his mind temporarily. Then I explained about the three tasks and said that an affidavit saying how clever Prince Alfred had been would be the best way of thanking him.

Prince Charming was only too happy to give us what we wanted and the next morning Prince Alfred and I got on the bike again and set off to tackle the other two tasks.

One evening we were riding along looking for a good place to spend the night when we came to the grounds of a great mansion. The gates were open and the place looked deserted so we rode in, hoping to find a nice cosy corner.

Before long we stumbled across somebody lying senseless on the ground. You didn't have to be very clever to guess who it was, though Prince Alfred still couldn't – he thought it was somebody in fancy dress. So I started to tell him that the chap was a prince who'd been changed into the Beast by a witch but, just then, we heard footsteps coming and barely had time to hide in the bushes before Beauty appeared.

She didn't look at all surprised when she saw the Beast lying there. She just said, "Here we go again," in a fed-up kind of way, stooped down and gave him a bit of a kiss. Everybody knows what happens next. Well, everybody except Prince Alfred that is; he gasped and said, "Crumbs, that was a good trick."

The Beast, or rather the ex-Beast as he now was, sat up and rubbed his knees. "You take longer to get back each time," he grumbled. "I'm starting to get rheumatism lying about in the damp and it's all your fault."

"I won't come back at all one of these times. I'll leave you lying here for ever," answered Beauty sulkily.

The girl was obviously bored stiff and in need of a change so I thought if we played our cards right we could polish off the second task there and then. Very respectfully, I whispered in Prince Alfred's ear, "I expect you're thinking that this is the girl who'd make a good queen, sir."

"No, Tyke," he said sadly. "She's married to that chap, you can tell by the way they speak to each other. Come on, let's go," and he started to creep away.

We weren't likely to get another chance like this so I did the first thing that came into my head. I picked up a clod of earth, aimed it at the ex-Beast and ducked back out of sight. Although I say it myself, it was a lovely shot, it hit him right on the ear. He spun around and saw Prince Alfred.

"Hey, you there, you blackguard," he cried as he drew his sword and leapt in pursuit. As he charged past my bush I stuck my foot out and he came a real cropper over it.

Prince Alfred came rushing back, looking very angry. "Who do you think you're calling names?" he shouted. "You're no gentleman, you don't deserve a smashing girl like this for a wife." And then he gazed at Beauty with a soppy look on his face.

"Actually," said Beauty in a matter-of-fact voice, "at this point in the story I'm not his wife."

That stumped Prince Alfred for a moment or two but part of what she said seemed to get through because the soppy look kind of oozed back on to his face. "Super . . . Fantastic . . ." he burbled and his ears went very pink. "In that case you could, um, sort of, I mean . . . er . . . in other words come away with . . . um . . . me . . . er . . . us."

"Right," said Beauty. "Let's get moving," and off we went.

The ex-Beast staggered to his feet and trotted after us. "Beauty," he whined, "you can't do this, it's not in the story."

"Bother the story," said Beauty. "It doesn't say in the story that you're beastlier when you're a prince than you are when you're the Beast. I'm not putting up with it any more, I'm going into another story. Goodbye."

The drive was steep so we picked up speed quickly. Soon the ex-Beast was left far behind and we saw no more of him.

It wasn't long before Prince Alfred was calling Beauty "old girl" and she was calling him "Alfie darling", and then one day Prince Alfred said to me, "I think you'd better start calling Beauty 'my lady' because a page can't go around calling a queen-to-be by her first name, can he?"

So it looked as if the second task was accomplished. All we had to do now was prove that Prince Alfred was brave.

It was a week before our chance came. We were passing through a village when we heard that a giant had just stolen the son of a rich merchant. We went to see the merchant, who lent us three horses so that we could pursue the giant and bring his little boy back.

We followed the giant's tracks and after a few hours saw a curious thing ahead of us. It turned out to be the great Beanstalk and there was Jack just starting to chop it down. We asked him if he'd seen a giant lately, at which he burst into tears.

"Yes," he snuffled. "I'm sorry if he's done any damage but it's not my fault." Then he blubbered on about how he always cut the Beanstalk down before the giant got to the bottom so that he fell and was killed.

But this time he'd somehow lost his axe and by the time he'd found it again the giant had reached the ground and gone rampaging off.

"He came back two hours ago," said Jack, cheering up. "He must be near the top by this time so if I cut it down now he'll be killed and the story will hardly be any different from what it usually is." He started chopping again.

Prince Alfred immediately ordered him to stop. "I'm going up after him," he said in a firm voice.

"*We* are going up after him," said Beauty in an even firmer voice. "You stay here, Tyke, and make sure no one cuts down the Beanstalk while we're gone." And with that they started to climb.

Three days went by and they didn't return. I started to get a bit worried and I thought I'd better pop up and see what was going on. I told Jack to take over my guard duties and started to climb the Beanstalk.

It was a lot higher than I'd thought. The whole day was spent climbing and when it got too dark to climb any more I ate the sandwiches which Jack's mother had made me and then curled up on a leaf and got some sleep. As soon as it was light enough I started climbing again and after two or three more hours I reached the top.

The first thing I saw was a huge cottage. It seemed a good place to start searching for my friends so I crept through the bushes right up to the door, which was standing ajar. Inside, two giants were talking while they ate their breakfast.

"His Lordship paid me five pieces of silver for 'em," boomed one giant. "He said they'd make nice toys for his young 'un to play with."

"You've been done," sneered the second giant. "Mannikins are worth twice as much as that. Why, they're delicacies, man."

"Go to the castle and tell him then and see where it gets you. He'll have you thrown in the moat," said the first giant and then he added sulkily, "Anyway, one of 'em was only half price because he was a little 'un."

Then they started to fall out over who should have the last sausage so I left.

I climbed to the top of a rocky outcrop and had a good look around. In the distance I saw the towers of a castle. It seemed a pretty good bet that

this was the one the giants had mentioned so I set off towards it at a jog-trot. When I arrived the drawbridge was down and the guards were gossiping, so I sneaked across without anybody seeing me.

When I entered the castle yard my heart sank. The walls and towers were so high they seemed to vanish into the clouds and there were doors and windows everywhere you looked. As for the stairs, I would have needed a ladder to get up just one step.

I thought it was going to take me years to find my friends in such a gigantic place but, as it turned out, it only took me a few minutes. That was because I suddenly remembered what the giant at the cottage had said about selling them as toys. Obviously the best thing to do was to look for the nursery. I'd hardly started looking before I spotted a clue.

It was standing on the sill of one of the lower windows and when the coast was clear I climbed up to it. It *was* the nursery and there, dressed up as toy soldiers, were my friends.

There wasn't anything I could do to rescue them at that moment so I hid in the ivy and waited for my chance. After what seemed like ages it came. The little giant was taken off somewhere and the nursery maid picked up my friends and put them away in a box with all the other toy soldiers. Then she went out and at last the nursery was empty. Very quietly I climbed into the room.

The lid of the box was much too heavy to lift by hand but I got around that all right and had my friends out in no time. They were jolly glad to see me, I can tell you, including little Bertie, the merchant's son.

But pleased as we all were to see each other again we didn't have time to stand about chatting. The nursery maid could have come back and caught us at any moment and then we'd all have been toy soldiers for life. So we tip-toed out of the nursery, clambered down a flight of stairs and crept into the courtyard. We had to cross this to get to the drawbridge but we hadn't gone very far before we ran into a big problem. The next few minutes after that weren't very nice at all.

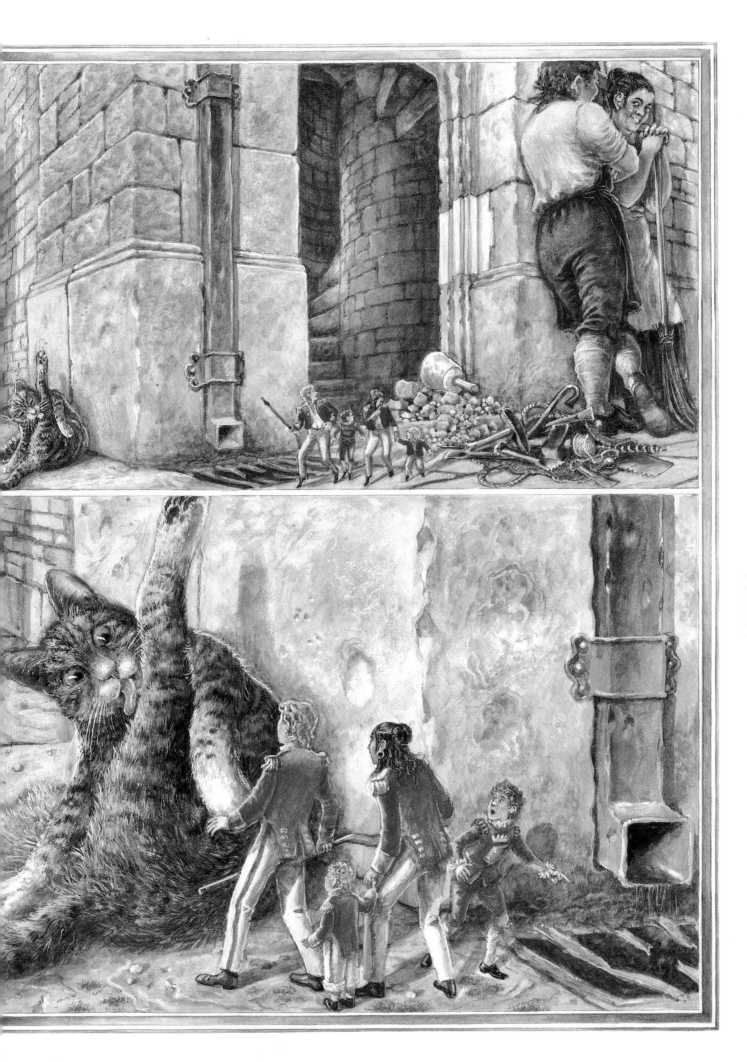

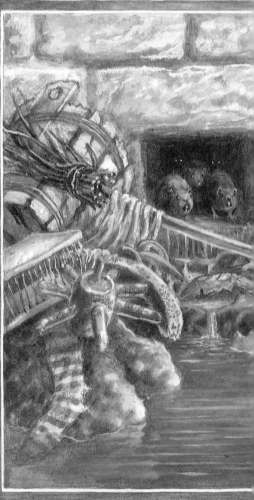

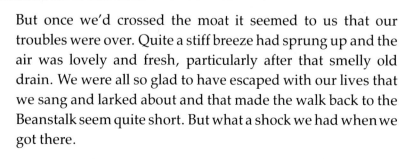

But once we'd crossed the moat it seemed to us that our troubles were over. Quite a stiff breeze had sprung up and the air was lovely and fresh, particularly after that smelly old drain. We were all so glad to have escaped with our lives that we sang and larked about and that made the walk back to the Beanstalk seem quite short. But what a shock we had when we got there.

The breeze had blown us away from the Beanstalk. Prince Alfred said that there was nothing to worry about, we could just make smoke signals and a passing helicopter would spot us. But Beauty said it would be a passing giant that did the spotting.

"Anyway," she said, "I've been watching that giantess at the cottage and that's given me a *sensible* idea."

It had been a long day and we were all very tired, but Beauty said there was still plenty of daylight left and we must use it: a wasted moment could mean the end for all of us. Then she explained her idea and we went to the giant's cottage to steal all the stuff we needed to carry it out. By the time it was dark everything was finished so we turned in and had a fairly good night's sleep.

I woke up early the next morning and went outside to stretch my legs, and it was a jolly good job I did, too. I raised the alarm and we just had time to prepare ourselves before the search party from the castle spotted us.

We got down from the giant's land a lot quicker than we got up, I can tell you. After we'd landed we walked back to the Beanstalk to get the horses. Then we said goodbye to Jack and set off for little Bertie's home.

His parents were very pleased to see him. In fact, the merchant said we could name our own reward so we told him the best reward he could give us was an affidavit saying that Prince Alfred had done a brave deed.

So now all the tasks were accomplished and we could go home. The merchant gave us three fine horses and let us each choose an outfit of clothes from his warehouse. After that he led us to a tunnel in the middle of a forest. He told us to ride in and take the seventh turning to the right and then the seventh to the left and that would lead us to our own country.

The tunnel ended in a place quite near the palace so in
another few minutes we were home. Prince Alfred went
straight to see the King in his study. Beauty and I waited
outside but we could hear the King shouting, "It's all lies
and forgeries." Then we were called into the study, too. The
King's face was purple with rage and he glared at us, growl-
ing like a wild beast. Beauty just curtsied and then, like a
good daughter-in-law-to-be, gave the King a big kiss. As if
by magic the scowls vanished from his face and he beamed.

Later, in his abdication speech, the King said that he'd
always thought Prince Alfred was an idle, irresponsible
blockhead but happily he'd been proved wrong. And now,
true to his promise and with the greatest confidence, he
placed the reins of government in his son's capable hands.

So Beauty and Prince Alfred were married and crowned
King and Queen and I became the youngest King's Equerry
and Confidential Advisor in the history of the world – and it
looks to me as if we stand a pretty good chance of living
happily ever after.

First published 1990 by
Macmillan Children's Books
A division of Macmillan Publishers Limited
London and Basingstoke
Associated Companies throughout the world.

Published simultaneously in Canada by
Collier Macmillan Canada, Inc.
1200 Eglintan Avenue East, Suite 200
Don Mills, Ontario
M3C 3NI

ISBN 0.02.953942.0

Printed in Belgium